Sleepover School

ROSIE BANKS

Wishing Star Palace

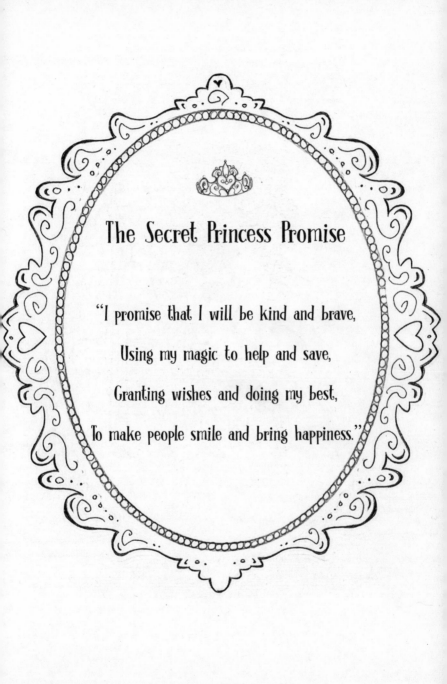

The Secret Princess Promise

"I promise that I will be kind and brave,

Using my magic to help and save,

Granting wishes and doing my best,

To make people smile and bring happiness."

CONTENTS

CHAPTER ONE

Bedtime Stories

"Pillow fight!" shouted Charlotte Williams, bashing her little brother Liam lightly on the head with a fluffy pillow.

"Oh no you don't!" giggled Liam, grabbing another pillow off his bed and flinging it at his sister.

Charlotte ducked, but Liam's twin brother Harvey swung a pillow at her back.

"Gotcha!" cried Harvey.

"Hey!" protested Charlotte, laughing. "Two against one isn't fair!"

"Oh yes it is!" cried Harvey, bouncing up and down on his bed. The duvet had rocket ships and stars on it, just like the one on Liam's bed. "You're bigger than us!"

"OK, then," said Charlotte, with a grin.

"You asked for it!" She tossed a pillow across the room at the exact moment the boys' bedroom door opened.

BOP! The pillow hit their dad right on the face!

"Oops!" said Charlotte. "Sorry, Dad!"

"Good shot," said Dad, chuckling. He was wearing an apron and had a tea towel slung over his shoulder. Picking up the pillow, Dad put it back on Liam's bed. "You lot need to settle down. It's nearly bedtime."

"Is Mum back from work yet?" asked Harvey.

"She's running late this evening," said Dad. "But she said to give you a kiss goodnight from her."

Charlotte's mum worked hard but she loved her new job. It was the reason they had moved to California from England not long ago.

"Aww," whined Liam. "But Mum always reads us a bedtime story."

"I'll read to you when I've finished tidying up the kitchen," said Dad.

"That's ages!" Harvey complained.

"I can read you guys a story," Charlotte offered.

"Thanks, Charlotte," said Dad, winking. "Goodnight, boys." Dad kissed the tops of Liam and Harvey's heads, then headed back downstairs.

"OK, guys," said Charlotte. "What should

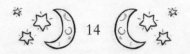

we read tonight?" She went over to the bookcase and ran her finger along the books' colourful spines. "How about this one?" she suggested, pulling a collection of fairy tales off the bookshelf.

"Yuck," said Liam, wrinkling his nose. "Fairy tales are always about princesses."

"Ugh," said Harvey, sticking out his tongue. "We don't want to read about boring old princesses."

"Who says princesses are boring?" Charlotte asked them.

"Me!" Liam and Harvey cried together. The boys burst out laughing.

"What about a princess who's also an astronaut?" said Charlotte.

Liam laughed. "Princesses can't be astronauts."

"Yeah," scoffed Harvey. "Princesses are silly and drippy."

"That's not true!" Charlotte said. She had to bite her lip to stop herself from telling her brothers that she had a friend who was a princess AND an astronaut! Princess Luna was cool and brave – and not the slightest bit silly or drippy! But Charlotte couldn't tell Liam and Harvey any of this, because Princess Luna was a

Secret Princess – and Charlotte had to keep the secret! Charlotte was one of the lucky few who knew about these special princesses who could grant wishes using magic. It was because Charlotte and her best friend Mia were training to become Secret Princesses, just like Luna!

"Earth to Charlotte!" said Harvey, waving his hand in front of Charlotte's face.

"Sorry," said Charlotte, snapping out of her daydream. "Why don't you two choose a book?"

Liam and Harvey searched through their bookcase.

"This one!" said Liam, pulling out a well-worn book. He handed Charlotte the copy

of *Spaceman Sam Saves the Day*.

Charlotte stifled a groan. She'd read this book to her brothers so many times she practically knew the story by heart!

The twins cuddled up on Liam's bed as Charlotte read them the story about an astronaut who landed on a planet that was made of jelly.

"'Then Spaceman Sam got back into his rocket and blasted back to Earth. The end,'" read Charlotte, shutting the book's tattered cover.

Liam yawned and rubbed his eyes as Harvey climbed into his own bed.

As the twins snuggled down under their duvets, Charlotte went over to the window.

18

Gazing out, she saw the silvery moon shining in the sky. *I wonder when Mia and I will earn our next moonstone*, Charlotte thought. To get their moonstone bracelets, she and Mia needed to earn three more moonstones by granting three wishes.

Charlotte glanced down at the gold necklace she was wearing under her pyjama top. A pearly white moonstone

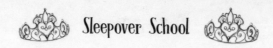

was embedded in the half-heart pendant. Soft moonlight streamed into the room, making Charlotte's necklace look like it was glowing. When she drew the curtains, Charlotte gasped. Her necklace was still glowing – but from magic, not moonlight!

"Night night," said Charlotte, quickly tucking her brothers into bed.

She hurried down the hall to her own bedroom, which had posters of her favourite gymnasts and pop stars on the walls. The top of her chest of drawers was cluttered with trophies from softball tournaments and medals from gymnastics competitions, while a framed picture of her and Mia hugging stood on her bedside table. Even though her best friend lived far away in England, Charlotte was about to go on an adventure with her!

Her heart racing with excitement, Charlotte held her pendant in her hand and murmured, "I wish I could see Mia."

The light shining out of the pendant grew brighter and brighter, making Charlotte's trophies and medals sparkle. Swirling around Charlotte, the magical light swept her far away from her bedroom.

She landed in the grounds of Wishing Star Palace. Her pyjamas had been replaced by a beautiful pink princess dress and her slippers had magically transformed into sparkling ruby slippers. Patting her head, Charlotte felt a diamond tiara resting on her brown curls. Only one star shone in the inky black sky. It was so dark Charlotte could barely make out the palace's four white turrets rising in the distance.

"Hi, Charlotte!"

Startled, Charlotte jumped. Peering through the gloom, she suddenly realised who the voice belonged to.

"Mia!" she cried, hugging her best friend. "It's so dark I didn't see you arrive."

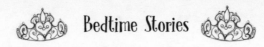

Mia tapped the sapphire ring on her finger and a light shone out of it, illuminating her long blonde hair and blue eyes. "There," she said, grinning. "That's better."

Mia was wearing a golden princess dress, but her tiara and ruby slippers were identical to Charlotte's.

"Good thinking," said Charlotte, tapping

her own sapphire ring to make more light.
The girls had recently earned their rings
for completing the previous stage of their
training. The rings warned them when
danger was near, but also came in handy
when they needed light.

"Who? Who?" came a voice in the dark.

"It's just us," said Charlotte loudly,
shining her ring around to see who it was.
"Mia and Charlotte."

"Who? Who?" the voice repeated.

"It's Mia and Charlotte!" the girls shouted
together.

But once again the mysterious voice
echoed in the dark …

"WHO? WHO?"

CHAPTER TWO
Lucky Owls

A group of Secret Princesses suddenly appeared in front of Charlotte and Mia. The glow from their magic sapphire rings surrounded them like a blue aura, lighting up the dark night. Like the girls, they wore beautiful dresses and tiaras – but the princesses also carried wands.

"Hi, girls," said Princess Ella, who had a

short, dark bob and was holding a pair of
binoculars. She had a pawprint symbol on
her necklace, because back in the real world
she was a vet.

"Were you calling to us?" asked Mia.

"Nope," said Princess Sylvie, shaking her
bright red curls. She had a pendant shaped
like a cupcake on her necklace because her

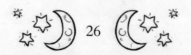

special talent was for baking.

"Has someone wished on another tiara star?" Charlotte asked hopefully.

The Tiara Constellation was a group of stars in the shape of a tiara. When it appeared in the sky, the Secret Princesses granted the first wish made on each of the four stars at the tiara's points. The powerful magic from these special wishes kept Wishing Star Palace hidden in the clouds for another year.

"Not yet," said Princess Ella. "We invited you here because we're going on a Night-time Nature Walk. We're hoping to see some nocturnal animals."

"Cool!" said Mia. She loved all animals.

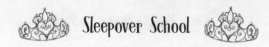

"You'll need some binoculars," said Sylvie. "I'll magic some up," said Princess Luna, who had short, dark, curly hair and a crescent moon pendant on her necklace, though it was green instead of gold. She waved her wand, but nothing happened. Luna sighed sadly. "I keep forgetting that my magic's not working."

"Don't worry, Luna," said Ella, patting her friend's shoulder reassuringly. "You'll get your magic back again soon. Mia and Charlotte have already started to break

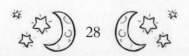

Princess Poison's horrid curse."

Princess Poison had once been a Secret Princess, but she'd been banished from Wishing Star Palace for ever – not that it stopped her from causing trouble! As cruel as the Secret Princesses were kind, Princess Poison used her magic to spoil wishes and get more power. When the Tiara Constellation had appeared in the sky, Princess Poison had blocked out the starlight with a thick, green mist. It had stopped Princess Luna's magic from working and turned her tiara, wand and necklace green. If Mia and Charlotte didn't grant three more tiara star wishes, Princess Luna would lose her magic for ever!

Just then, the mysterious cry rang out
again.

"WHO? WHO?"

"Oh good," said Ella. "That was a Lucky
Owl! Let's find it!"

Mia and Charlotte glanced at each other,
relieved. It had been an owl calling them in
the dark!

"Wait!" said Sylvie. "What about Alice?"

"Let me check where she is," said Ella. She
tapped her moonstone bracelet and spoke
into the gem. "Hi, Alice," she said. "Are
you coming? The girls are here."

"Sorry to keep you waiting!" said a
princess with strawberry-blonde hair,
suddenly appearing out of nowhere.

The magical ruby slippers that had transported her sparkled on her feet. "I was working on a new song and lost track of time." Princess Alice hugged Mia and Charlotte. "How are my favourite trainee princesses?"

Back in the real world, Princess Alice was the pop star Alice de Silver. But Mia and Charlotte had known her since before she was famous, when Alice was their babysitter. It was Alice who had spotted their potential to become Secret Princesses

and given them their magic necklaces.

Ella held a finger to her lips. "Keep your voices low so we don't scare the animals."

With the princesses' rings glowing like torches, they walked quietly through the dark palace grounds.

"Look!" whispered Luna, as a flash of

fiery orange streaked past, followed by a
four smaller streaks. With a rustling noise,
the orange lights disappeared into the
undergrowth.

"What was that?" asked Charlotte.

"A fire fox and her babies," explained
Ella. "When they run, their fur crackles
with magical energy."

"Wow!" breathed Mia.

They moved on, walking deeper into a
wooded glade.

"Lucky Owls usually perch around here,"
said Ella quietly. "You two can help me
look." She waved her wand, and suddenly
Mia and Charlotte each had a pair of
binoculars around their neck.

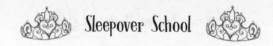
Charlotte looked through her binoculars, scanning the treetops overhead. "I think I see one!" she whispered, spotting an owl with white feathers perched on a tree branch.

"He's gorgeous," said Mia softly, peering through her own binoculars.

"Why are they called Lucky Owls?" wondered Charlotte.

"If you spot one when there's a full moon it brings you good luck," explained Princess Ella, smiling.

As the owl hooted and soared into the moonlit sky, Charlotte noticed a second star shining through Princess Poison's mist. The owl had brought them good luck already!

"Someone's made a wish on the second tiara star!" she exclaimed.

"Can we grant it?" asked Mia.

"Of course," said Alice.

"Maybe the owl's good luck will help us grant the wish," said Charlotte.

"I hope so," said Luna.

"We won't let anything stop us," Mia promised the princess.

Mia and Charlotte clicked the heels of their ruby slippers together three times. "The Astronomy Tower!" they cried.

Their magic slippers whisked them to a room at the top of one of the palace's towers. A huge gold telescope stood in the middle, pointing out of the window.

Mia looked through the lens. "Oh dear," she said.

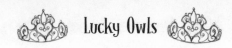

"The girl we need to help looks very sad."

Charlotte looked through the telescope and saw a girl with long, straight black hair. She was carrying a red suitcase and looked a bit lost. A message suddenly appeared on the glass. She read it out loud:

"Touch the telescope to see a star.
Call out Ashley's name and you'll go far."

Mia and Charlotte gripped the telescope and cried, "Ashley!"

The girls were suddenly whisked away. As they spiralled through the night sky, sparkling stars and glowing comets flashing past them at the speed of light.

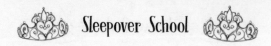

A moment later, they arrived outside an old brick building covered in ivy. They were wearing the same school uniform as all the other kids.

"Let's go in," Charlotte said boldly, pulling the door open.

They entered a hall filled with boys and girls queuing with their parents. The wood-panelled walls were decorated with portraits of headteachers and colourful banners with dragons on them.

"Welcome to Dearborn Academy," said an older girl with a name badge that said 'Rory'. She gave them sticky labels to write their names on. "You can go and register over there."

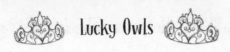

"Is that her?" whispered Mia, sticking on her name badge. A girl with long black hair stood at the end of one of the queues clutching the handle of a red wheelie suitcase.

"Let's find out," said Charlotte, joining the queue. The girl turned around and smiled at them, revealing a gap in her front teeth. It was Ashley!

"Hi … Charlotte," said the girl, reading Charlotte's name badge. Peering at Mia's badge, she said, "Hi, Mia."

Charlotte pretended to read Ashley's name badge. "Hi, Ashley."

"Are you with your parents?" Ashley asked them.

"Er, no," said Mia.

"Me neither," said Ashley. "I'm glad I'm not the only one."

"Where are your parents?" Charlotte asked curiously.

"In Hong Kong, where we live," explained Ashley. "My dad's job means that we move a lot. My parents decided I should go to boarding school so I don't have to keep

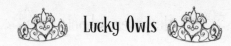

switching schools all the time."

Aha! thought Charlotte. Dearborn
Academy was a boarding school!

"Are you excited about going to boarding
school?" Mia asked.

"I was looking forward to midnight feasts
and fun things like that," said Ashley. "But
so far I just feel homesick and out of place."

Charlotte smiled sympathetically. "My family moved to a different country not long ago. I soon settled in."

"I wish I could fit in here," said Ashley, sighing.

Charlotte caught Mia's eye and she gave a tiny nod in reply. They had discovered Ashley's wish!

"I'm sure you'll soon feel right at home," said Mia encouragingly.

Ashley gazed at the other students apprehensively. "It's hard to believe that I'll ever have friends here," she said.

"You have two already," said Charlotte, grinning. "Me and Mia!"

CHAPTER THREE
Moving In

When Ashley got to the front of the queue, a lady ticked her name off a list and gave her an information pack. "You're in Wayland House," she said, handing Ashley a key. "Your roommate is called Zoe Gibbs."

"Well, I suppose I should go to my dormitory and unpack," said Ashley. "It was nice to meet you both."

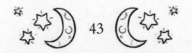

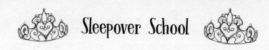

"Want us to come and help you?" Charlotte offered quickly.

"That would be great," said Ashley. She took a campus map out of her information pack. "You can help me find Wayland House."

They wandered through the leafy green campus, passing lots of other old brick buildings, until they found Ashley's dormitory. The door was propped open as girls and their parents carried suitcases and boxes from their cars into the building.

"This is my room," said Ashley, opening a door with a number seven on it.

The room was empty except for two single beds, two desks and two chests of drawers.

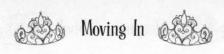

The walls, painted a stark white, were completely bare.

Ashley sank down on one of the beds. "My bedroom at home was lovely," she said glumly. "But this is horrible. It feels like a prison cell!"

"Let's get you unpacked," said Mia. "Then it will feel more like home."

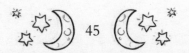

"It won't take long," said Ashley, unzipping her suitcase. "I could only take one bag on the aeroplane."

Mia helped Ashley put her clothes in the chest of drawers, while Charlotte helped by making the bed.

Ashley unpacked a book, a flute and a jewellery box, putting them on her desk next to a framed photo of her family.

"Oh, I love that book," said Mia, spotting the cover. "There's a boarding school in that, isn't there?"

"Yes," said Ashley miserably. "Everyone has midnight feasts and lots of fun. But Dearborn Academy doesn't seem anything like the Magic Boarding School so far."

She took out an old teddy bear and put it
on her pillow.

"Who's that?" asked Charlotte.

"It's Bobo. I've
had him since
I was tiny,"
said Ashley.
"I hope my
roommate
doesn't think
I'm too
babyish for
bringing a soft toy."

"Don't worry, I have a special teddy, too,"
Mia confided.

"Hey," said Charlotte, thinking of a joke.

"Why aren't teddy bears ever hungry?"

"Because they're stuffed!" answered someone holding a big box. She came into the room and set the box down on the floor, revealing a happy freckled face with a friendly grin.

"You must be Ashley," said the girl, pushing frizzy blonde hair out of her face. "I'm Zoe. We're going to be roommates!"

"Hi," said Ashley. "These are my friends Mia and Charlotte."

Zoe's parents followed her into the bedroom, loaded down with boxes and suitcases. They introduced themselves, then busied themselves unpacking Zoe's belongings and putting things away.

Zoe took out a cuddly purple monkey and placed it on her pillow. She grinned at Ashley. "I couldn't leave Chimpy at home."

Ashley smiled back shyly.

"I hope you'll keep your room tidy," said Zoe's dad.

"Yes, Dad," said Zoe, rolling her eyes as she stuck posters of pop stars on the walls.

"Look!" whispered Mia, nudging Charlotte's arm.

One of the posters showed Alice looking very glamorous in a glittery minidress. Charlotte grinned at Mia. Zoe clearly had excellent taste in music!

"Come on, Zoe," said her mum. "We've got to get the rest of the stuff from the car."

When Zoe and her parents headed out of the room, Ashley picked up the picture of her family and sighed. "I really miss my mum and dad."

"I'm sure they miss you too," said Mia soothingly.

"Zoe seems really nice," Charlotte said.

Ashley nodded and looked over at the other side of the room. Even though Zoe hadn't finished unpacking, her side of the

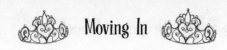

room was already full of her belongings. It made Ashley's side look very bare in comparison. The only bit of colour on the walls was a spot of blue light.

Wait a second ... thought Charlotte. The light was coming from Mia's sapphire ring. Pulling her hand out of her pocket, Charlotte saw that her own ring was flashing, too!

"Mia!" she whispered. "We're in danger!"

Before Mia could reply, there was a loud rap on the door. Without waiting for a reply, a short, tubby man barged into the bedroom.

"Room inspection!" he announced. It was Hex, Princess Poison's horrible assistant!

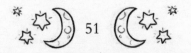

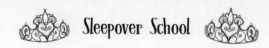

Hex marched around the bedroom, shaking his head. "Tut tut," he said. "This is all against the rules."

RIP! He tore the poster of Alice off the wall, ripping it in half. Then he yanked Zoe's other posters off the wall.

"Stop it! Get out!" Charlotte ordered Hex angrily, but he just ignored her.

YANK! Hex pulled open the drawers and flung out all Ashley and Zoe's clothes.

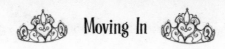

He ripped the duvets off their beds and chucked their soft toys on the ground.

"Bobo!" gasped Ashley.

"Stop that!" shouted Mia, running over to pick up the teddy.

SMASH! Hex threw the picture of Ashley's family on the floor, shattering the glass in the frame.

"No!" cried Ashley.

Hex picked up the book and ripped out a handful of pages. "Don't think boarding school is going to be like your story book," he said nastily, scattering the pages on the floor. "You're NEVER going to fit in here!"

With that he went out of the room, slamming the door behind him.

"Oh no," wailed Ashley, looking at the mess. "Why did he do that? Zoe's going to think I trashed our room. She'll never be friends with me now." She curled up on her mattress and sobbed.

Charlotte could hear footsteps coming down the hall.

"Quick, Mia!" she said. "We need to fix this before Zoe and her parents come back."

Mia ran over and held her glowing half-heart pendant next to Charlotte's.

"I wish for Ashley and Zoe's room to be cool and cosy," Mia said.

Brilliant golden light poured out of the heart, transforming the room. Now there were matching pink and pale green duvet

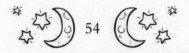

covers on the beds and a fluffy pink rug on the floor. Posters of pop stars hung on the walls and twinkling flower-shaped fairy lights stretched across the room. The girls' cuddly toys rested on two comfy beanbag chairs next to a little bookcase filled with books, and a collage of family photos hung over each girl's bed. Pop music was playing softly on a speaker.

Hearing the music, Ashley look up from her tear-stained pillow. She blinked and rubbed her eyes, looking around her room in astonishment.

"How did you do that?" Ashley asked in amazement.

But there was no time to explain.

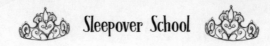

"I'm back!" said Zoe, returning with a violin case. She looked around the room, her expression unreadable.

Uh oh, thought Charlotte. What if Zoe didn't like how the magic had changed the room?

To Charlotte's relief, a big grin spread across Zoe's face. "I love how our room looks!" she said.

CHAPTER FOUR
A Big Crash

As one of Alice's pop hits started playing, all the girls grinned. "I love Alice de Silver!" exclaimed Zoe, dropping her violin case on her bed. "Do you like classical music, too?"

"Yes," said Ashley. "I play the flute."

"Cool!" said Zoe. "Maybe we can both

join the school orchestra." The roommates grinned at each other.

"Knock knock," said Zoe's dad, carrying a box into the room.

"That's the last of your stuff, Zoe," said Zoe's mum. She gazed around approvingly. "Your room looks great."

"We'd better head off," said Zoe's dad. "We've got a long journey ahead of us."

"It's very nice to meet you, Ashley," said Zoe's mum. "Keep an eye on Zoe for us, won't you?"

"I will," said Ashley, smiling.

"I'll come out with you to say goodbye," said Zoe, walking with her parents out of the room.

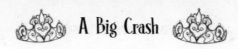

As soon as the door had shut behind them, Ashley spun round to face Mia and Charlotte. "Am I dreaming?" she asked. "What just happened was like … magic or something!"

"It *was* magic," admitted Charlotte. "Mia and I aren't really students here. We're training to become Secret Princesses and we've come here to help grant your wish of fitting in."

"Our necklaces let us use magic to make three small magic wishes," said Mia.

"I've never heard of Secret Princesses," said Ashley. "Is that because I grew up in a different country?"

"No," said Mia, shaking her head.

"Most people haven't heard about Secret Princesses – only the people whose wishes they're trying to grant."

"Nobody else even notices the magic," added Charlotte.

"Oh," said Ashley. "That's why Zoe and her parents didn't think it was strange that our room looked completely different."

Her brow suddenly wrinkled. "But who was that horrible man who made the mess?"

"His name is Hex," said Mia. "He works for someone called Princess Poison."

"Is she a Secret Princess?" asked Ashley.

"No way," said Charlotte. "She spoils wishes instead of granting them."

"Don't worry, though," Mia said quickly. "We won't let her ruin your wish."

Zoe came back into the room. She was sniffling and her eyes looked red. "Sorry," she said, her voice cracking. "It was hard to say goodbye."

"I miss my family too," admitted Ashley.

"We'll just have to help each other when we feel homesick," said Zoe, bravely.

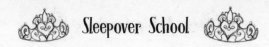

Ashley, Mia and Charlotte helped Zoe unpack the rest of her boxes. Soon, all of her belongings had been tidied away.

"What should we do now?" Zoe wondered.

Ashley took out her information pack. "There's a campus tour starting in a few minutes," she said, reading the schedule.

"Let's head over now," said Zoe. "Otherwise we'll never learn our way around this place."

The four girls hurried back to the hall where they'd registered. A group of students had formed outside the door.

"Hi," said Rory, the older girl who had given Mia and Charlotte name badges earlier. "I'm going to be your guide today.

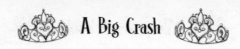

I'm in my final year and I'm here to help you settle in to the school."

They set off down the hallways. "This is where you'll have science classes," Rory told them, taking them to a classroom with gleaming microscopes and a model skeleton. "The skeleton's nickname is Mr Bones."

Ashley and Zoe giggled.

Rory led the group to a classroom filled with easels and paints. Beautiful artwork by students hung on the walls. There was even a pottery wheel for making ceramics.

"This is the art studio," Rory informed the group.

"Art's my best subject," Ashley told Zoe.

"Mine too!" exclaimed Zoe.

Next, Rory took the group to the library. There were endless shelves of books, comfy armchairs to curl up in, and long wooden tables for doing homework.

"Mmm," said Mia, inhaling deeply. "I love the smell of books."

"Have you read this?" Ashley asked Zoe,

pulling a copy of *The Magic Boarding School* off a shelf.

"That's my favourite book!" said Zoe. "It's the whole reason I wanted to come to boarding school!"

The roommates grinned at each other, pleased to discover that they had so much in common.

After they had explored the library, Rory

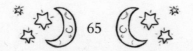

led them across a lush green lawn.

"Who's that?" asked Ashley as they passed
a statue of a dragon near the school gates.

"Oh, that's our mascot,"
explained Rory.

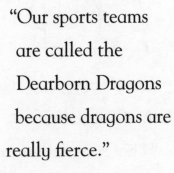

"Our sports teams
are called the
Dearborn Dragons
because dragons are
really fierce."

"But dragons aren't
fierce at all!" Mia whispered
to Charlotte.

Charlotte nodded, remembering the
lovely purple dragon they had once met at
Wishing Star Palace. They had watched

the gentle dragon's eggs hatch and even got
to name the babies!

Rory led the tour group to a tall brick
tower with a clock at its top. "This is the
clocktower," she said, heading up the stairs.
"It's where the Astronomy Club meets.
There's a really good view from the top."

The Astronomy Tower at Wishing Star
Palace suddenly flashed through Charlotte's
mind. They really needed to grant Ashley's
wish so that Luna could get her magic back!

She glanced back at Mia and saw a
worried look on her face.

"Are you thinking about Luna, too?"
whispered Charlotte to her friend as they
climbed up the stairs.

Mia nodded, too out of breath to reply.

"I'm sure we'll grant Ashley's wish," said Charlotte. "She and Zoe are getting along really well."

"But Hex was here," murmured Mia. "That means Princess Poison is going to try to spoil Ashley's wish."

"We'll be ready for her," said Charlotte defiantly.

From the top of the clocktower, the campus stretched out far beneath them, a patchwork of green playing fields, a blue pond and red brick buildings.

"Wow!" gasped Ashley, looking down.

Rory smiled. "Isn't it lovely? We're so lucky to go to school here."

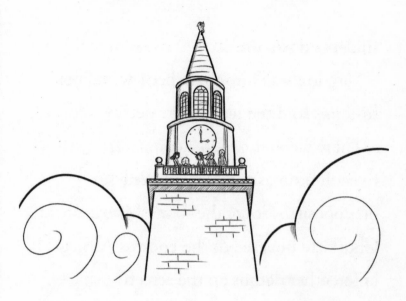

The clock struck three times. It was so loud everyone jumped.

"It's three o'clock," said Rory. "You need to go to the Computer Centre now."

They trooped back downstairs and Rory directed them to a modern building nearby. The Computer Centre had rows and rows of computers. A teacher gave each of the new

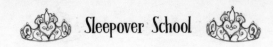

students a password.

"Try logging into the school's computer system," said the teacher.

There weren't two free computers next to each other, so Ashley and Zoe sat on opposite sides of the room. Mia and Charlotte hovered at the back as Ashley entered her details on the screen.

"Uh oh," said Mia.

Charlotte looked up and saw a small white robot wheeling over to Ashley, its green eyes flashing. It wasn't part of the school's computer centre, it was EVA – Princess Poison's Extra Villainous Assistant! On their last adventure, Princess Poison had cursed the robot to obey her commands!

Before they could warn Ashley, the robot
stopped at Ashley's computer and pressed
several keys before gliding away noiselessly.

Ashley's computer started beeping loudly.
"Oh no," said Ashley. "My computer's not
working."

"Mia, you're good with computers," said
Charlotte. "Can you fix it?"

"I can try," said Mia. She went over to Ashley and crouched down beside her. "I'm going to try to restart your computer." Mia held down a few buttons on the keyboard but nothing happened. "Hmm. That's odd."

"Mine's crashed too," complained the boy next to Ashley.

"And mine," said another girl, clicking her mouse in frustration.

Every computer screen in the room had turned black. A message in neon green flashed up on Ashley's screen, saying: "VIRUS WARNING."

The teacher tried to restart the computers. Nothing worked – all the screens remained blank. "You must have clicked on a virus,"

she told Ashley. "Now all of the computers have been infected."

"But I didn't do anything," said Ashley. "It was the robot!"

"What robot?" the teacher asked, puzzled.

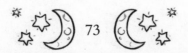

"That robot—" Ashley looked around frantically. But EVA was nowhere to be seen!

CHAPTER FIVE
A Spoilsport

"The Computer Centre doesn't have robots," said the teacher, frowning. "And at Dearborn Academy we don't approve of telling tall tales."

"But—" protested Ashley.

"We encourage students to take full responsibility for their actions," said the teacher, giving Ashley a stern look.

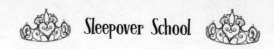

The other students stared at Ashley and muttered amongst themselves.

"This is terrible," whispered Charlotte. "We can't let Ashley get the blame for something she didn't do."

"We need to use another wish," said Mia.

Charlotte held her pendant up to Mia's necklace. "I wish that the computer virus would become a fun computer game," she said quickly.

Brilliant light filled the Computer Centre and suddenly all of the computers were working again. The black screens had been replaced by a game with brightly coloured graphics and jolly music. Soon, Ashley and the other students were happily playing.

"Woo hoo! I just got to the next level," boasted a boy sitting near Ashley.

"OK, you can all log off now," said the teacher.

"Aww!" complained the students. "But this game is awesome!"

As everyone got up to leave, Ashley rushed over to Mia and Charlotte. "Did you two do more magic?" she whispered.

"Yes," said Mia. "We knew the virus wasn't your fault."

"So I wasn't imagining that robot?" said Ashley.

"No," said Charlotte. "The robot was real. It's another one of Princess Poison's mean assistants."

Ashley shuddered. "Princess Poison must be really horrible if her helpers are that mean," she said, her eyes wide.

Mia and Charlotte exchanged looks. They hoped that Ashley wouldn't have to find out just how nasty the princess could be!

As they left the Computer Centre, Zoe joined them and said, "That computer game was cool, wasn't it?"

"Listen up, everyone!" called Rory, waving her hand in the air to get their attention. "We're heading out to the sports field now to play some team-building games."

They followed the older girl to the sports

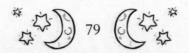

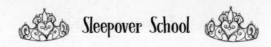
field, which was next to the pond they'd seen from the clocktower.

"First we're going to play Dragon Tag," announced Rory.

The older girl divided the new students into two teams. "You're going to be the head of the dragon," she told Ashley. Mia, Charlotte and the other kids on Ashley's team joined hands in a long chain with Zoe at the end. "You're the dragon's tail," said Rory, tucking a handkerchief into Zoe's pocket.

Once she'd arranged the other team, Rory said, "The dragon's head must try and capture the other team's tail. But you can't let go of each other's hands."

Soon, everyone was laughing breathlessly
as the two 'dragons' chased each other
across the grass. Charlotte's right hand
clung to Mia and her left hand gripped
Ashley's as they dodged away from the
other team.

Someone on the other team almost
fell over, and their dragon slowed down.
Seeing her team's chance, Ashley surged
forward, pulling the rest of the dragon along
with her.

"Go, Ashley!" cried Charlotte.

"You can do it!" shouted Zoe.

Ashley reached forward, stretching out
her free hand. "Got it!" she cried, waving

a red hanky in the air. She'd captured the dragon's tail!

"Yay!" cheered Mia.

BREEET! BREEET!

Hex marched over, blowing a whistle. He was wearing a tight Dearborn Academy tracksuit. Charlotte groaned.

"That girl was cheating!" Hex said, pointing at Ashley.

Ashley frowned. "No, I wasn't—"

BREEET! Hex gave another shrill blast on his whistle, cutting her off.

Charlotte wondered whether she and Mia needed to use another wish, but before she could say anything, Ashley's teammates rushed to her defence.

"She was NOT cheating!" Zoe insisted.

"Yeah!" said a girl on their team.

The other kids on Ashley's team nodded.

"OK, let's play a different game," suggested Rory. "It's called a Trust Walk. Everybody find a partner."

"Will you be my partner?" Ashley quickly asked Zoe.

"Of course," replied Zoe.

"Roommates aren't allowed to be partners," Hex said, cutting in between them. "Pair up with someone else."

Zoe shrugged and asked another girl to be partners.

Ashley looked around anxiously. By now, all the other kids had found partners.

"I'll be your partner," Charlotte offered quickly, sure Mia wouldn't mind.

"No!" said Hex, smirking. "*I'll* be her partner. I know how you two love working together."

Before Charlotte could protest, Rory came over and tied a blindfold over Ashley's eyes. "Your partner will guide you around."

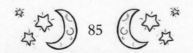

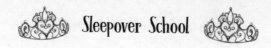
"Stay close to Ashley," Charlotte whispered as Mia tied a blindfold over her eyes. "I'm sure Hex is up to no good."

With the blindfold on, Charlotte could only see black. For a moment, she felt scared until Mia gently took her arm.

"Don't worry, Charlotte," Mia said. "I've got you."

As Mia led her around, Charlotte didn't feel worried even though she couldn't see a thing. She trusted her best friend completely. Unfortunately, Ashley's partner couldn't be trusted at all!

Mia gently steered Charlotte to the left. "Uh oh. Hex is leading Ashley over towards the pond."

Clinging to Mia's arm, Charlotte
stumbled along as fast as she could.

There was a splash, followed by a shriek.

"What was that?" Charlotte asked.

"Ashley," said Mia grimly.

Tearing off her blindfold, Charlotte saw
Ashley standing knee-deep in the cold,
muddy water.

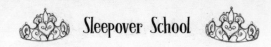

"You led me into the water on purpose," Ashley accused Hex.

"You didn't follow my directions," said Hex smugly. "Maybe you're not cut out for Dearborn Academy."

As Charlotte and Mia hauled Ashley out of the water, Rory called out, "Meet at the dining hall at six o'clock for the Welcome Feast. Everyone can dress up however they like!"

"Everything's going wrong for me," said Ashley miserably. "I don't even want to go to the feast."

"That's exactly what Hex wants," said Charlotte.

"You mustn't let him win," said Mia.

"Oh no," said Zoe, spotting Ashley's wet legs. "What happened?"

"Her partner was a spoilsport," said Mia.

"Come on," said Zoe, putting her arm around Ashley's shoulder. "Let's go back to our dorm. We can get ready for the Welcome Feast together."

Back at the dorm, Ashley changed out of her wet clothes.

"Want me to plait your hair?" Zoe offered.

"Thanks," said Ashley, sitting down on a beanbag.

As Zoe deftly plaited Ashley's hair, other girls who lived on their corridor came in to introduce themselves. Zoe got out a tin of cookies her mum had baked and soon the

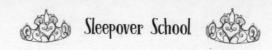
room was filled with girls munching biscuits and listening to pop music.

"This is so much fun!" said Zoe.

"Maybe we can all have a midnight feast later on," suggested Ashley hopefully.

Charlotte and Mia grinned at each other. Ashley was starting to have fun!

"Speaking of food," said Zoe, "we'd better head over to the dining hall! It's time for the Welcome Feast!"

CHAPTER SIX
The Welcome Feast

Linking arms, they headed across the campus with the other girls from the dorm.

"My mum's a really good cook," said Ashley. "I'm going to miss her food."

"It's my dad who cooks in our family," said Zoe. "His lasagne is the best."

"In *The Magic Boarding School*, the food always sounds amazing," said Mia.

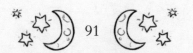

"Yeah," agreed Charlotte. "They're always having midnight feasts with yummy things like pumpkin puffs."

"And magic gummy sweets," said Zoe.

"Washed down with fizzy creamy-ale," said Ashley. Her tummy let out a growl.

Zoe grinned at Ashley and winked. "I'm really hungry too!"

The candlelit dining hall had long wooden tables set with gleaming plates. Banners with the school houses' crests hung from the ceiling and old-fashioned paintings in heavy gold frames showed teachers wearing academic robes.

The girls took their places in a line of students queueing up for food.

Staff members in white aprons and chef's hats served up plates of roast beef smothered in gravy, creamy mashed potatoes and crisp vegetables.

"Mmm," said Ashley, sniffing the air. "The food here might not be magical but it smells great."

"Ashley seems really happy," Mia whispered as Ashley chatted to the other kids from their dorm.

"I know," said Charlotte. "I'm sure we can grant her wish."

"Don't count your chickens before they're hatched," hissed a mean-sounding voice behind them. "Haven't your princess friends taught you that?"

Charlotte spun around and saw a tall, thin woman in a green dress and spiky high heels. Her hair was as black as midnight, except for a streak of white, and she wore a necklace with a poison bottle pendant around her scrawny neck. EVA was by her side, holding Princess Poison's wand.

"Ugh," said Mia, pulling a face.

"I've just lost my appetite."

"That's handy," said Princess Poison, narrowing her eyes at the girls. "Because Ashley's about to lose her appetite too." She held out her hand impatiently. "EVA, my wand!"

Raising its arm stiffly, the robot handed Princess Poison her wand.

"I'm going to make this the most Unwelcoming Feast Dearborn Academy has ever had," Princess Poison chortled gleefully. "It will be so terrible that Ashley will be desperate to go back home."

Pointing her wand at the food, Princess Poison rasped out a spell:

This welcome feast makes me sick,
So I'll spoil it with a nasty trick!

Princess Poison waved her wand, unleashing a shower of green sparks that swirled through the air and landed on the food just as Ashley reached the front of the line. The spell transformed the feast, making all the food look disgusting!

Ashley gulped as a dinner lady spooned lumpy sludge on to her plate. *PLOP!*

Plonking a piece of gristly grey meat on top of the sludge, the lady asked, "Do you want veg with that?"

"Er, no thanks," said Ashley, looking at the bowl of slimy-looking greens.

"Don't forget dessert," grunted the dinner lady, dumping a small bowl of wobbling green jelly with bits floating inside it on Ashley's tray.

"What is it?" asked Ashley.

"My special Lime Jelly Surprise!" crowed Princess Poison. "Enjoy!" she said, sauntering off.

"Ew," said Zoe, peering at the green jelly.

"I think there are mushrooms and prawns in this jelly!"

Ashley started carrying her tray across the dining hall, looking for a place to sit. Instead of sparkling with candlelight, the dining hall looked dingy and gloomy now. The wooden tables had become plastic, with cracked, uncomfortable chairs.

Suddenly, EVA took off, wheeling across the dining room floor at top speed.

CRASH! The robot bashed right into Ashley.

SMASH! Ashley dropped her tray. Her plate and cup shattered on the floor, splattering grey gruel and green jelly all over the place.

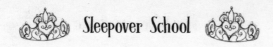

"What a clumsy girl," sneered Princess Poison loudly.

"Go home!" jeered Hex.

"HA! HA! HA!" Under Princess Poison's spell, all of the students in the dining hall laughed nastily and pointed at Ashley. Her cheeks blazed bright pink with embarrassment and she looked like she was about to burst into tears.

"We've got to do something, Mia!"
Charlotte shouted over the roars of
laughter.

"Let's use our last wish!" Mia replied.

The girls held their necklaces together.
Their half-heart pendants glowed very
faintly, as there was only enough magic left
for one more wish.

"I wish for Ashley to have an amazing
midnight feast," said
Charlotte.

Their necklaces
gave a flash of magical
light. Instantly,
the dining hall was
transformed.

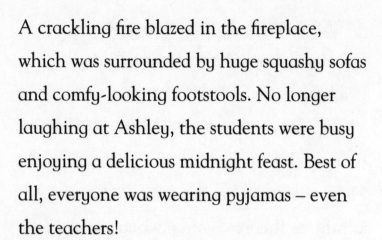

A crackling fire blazed in the fireplace, which was surrounded by huge squashy sofas and comfy-looking footstools. No longer laughing at Ashley, the students were busy enjoying a delicious midnight feast. Best of all, everyone was wearing pyjamas – even the teachers!

"Great idea, Charlotte," said Mia, who was now wearing a fleecy dressing gown over pretty polka-dotted pyjamas.

"Thanks," said Charlotte, who had on a pink and black leopard-print onesie.

"Thank you so much," said Ashley, who was wearing a flannel nightgown and fluffy slippers. "Was that Princess Poison?"

"The one and only," Charlotte confirmed.

"I thought her helpers were bad," said Ashley, "but she's much worse."

"Enjoy the feast with your friends," said Mia. "Leave worrying about Princess Poison to us."

"You come too," said Ashley. Mia and Charlotte followed her to where her new friends were roasting sausages on long forks over the roaring fire.

When their sausages were sizzling and brown, the girls helped themselves to baked beans and jacket potatoes topped with melted cheese. They all sat down on a sofa and tucked in to the feast.

"This is amazing!" said Ashley, munching on a sausage.

"Does anyone want some ginger beer?" asked Zoe, pouring out glasses.

Charlotte just nodded, her mouth full.

"I'm stuffed," said a girl from Ashley's dorm, patting her belly.

"Not me," said Zoe, pointing across the room. "Have you seen what's for dessert?"

"Oh my gosh!" said Ashley. "There's an ice cream sundae bar!"

Ashley and her friends ran over to make sundaes. There were six different flavours of ice cream to choose from and every topping imaginable – from caramel and coconut to sprinkles and strawberries!

Charlotte helped herself to a scoop of chocolate, then drizzled sauce on top.

Princess Poison and Hex sidled up as she
sprinkled on hundreds and thousands.

"Oh dear," said Charlotte sarcastically.
"There's no Lime Jelly Surprise left."

"That's fine with me," said Princess Poison
smugly. "Because I know something else
that's all gone – your magic."

"We don't need magic to grant Ashley's wish," said Mia, topping her strawberry sundae with swirls of whipped cream. "She's made lots of friends and is happy already."

"That won't last long," said Princess Poison. "Will it, Hex?"

"GLWUMPH," mumbled Hex through a mouthful of mint chocolate chip ice cream.

"Gah!" shrieked Princess Poison in frustration. She threw Hex's sundae on the floor, then waved her wand. They both vanished in a flash of green light.

Charlotte grinned at Mia. "I guess Princess Poison doesn't like mint chocolate chip."

CHAPTER SEVEN
The Lantern Ceremony

After eating their fill of ice cream, Ashley and her new friends chatted and played board games in front of the roaring fire. Mia and Charlotte joined in, but kept their eyes peeled for Princess Poison and her helpers. They were sure they hadn't seen the last of them.

DONG! DONG! DONG! The clocktower

bell was ringing.

"It's time to go outside for the Lantern Ceremony," announced Rory, coming into the dining hall. "That's when new students officially become a part of Dearborn Academy."

"But we're in our pyjamas," protested one of Ashley's dorm-mates.

"That's all part of the tradition!" said Rory, smiling.

Mia and Charlotte looked at each other and giggled. No one had noticed the magic – in fact they thought they were meant to be wearing pyjamas!

Outside, the sky was completely black. Following Rory, the new students shuffled

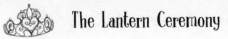

across the dark campus in their slippers.
The buildings looked cosy and welcoming
with lights glowing in the windows. As they
approached the school gates, they heard
singing.

"Oh my gosh!" gasped Ashley.

On the other side of the gates, older
students lined the path holding lanterns
and sang the school song. At the end of the
path was the dragon statue.

"Walk through the gates and pat the dragon's head for good luck," Rory instructed. "Then you'll get a lantern, meaning you've officially joined the school."

"This is so cool!" said Zoe, clutching Ashley's arm excitedly.

Ashley nodded, her eyes shining.

One by one, the new students walked through the gates and down the path. As they rubbed the dragon statue's head, the older students cheered and handed them each a lantern.

"Good luck," said Mia as Zoe walked through the gates.

"Yes, good luck," said Princess Poison,

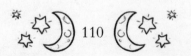

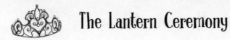

suddenly appearing with Hex and EVA. "I hope you aren't afraid of dragons."

"What do you mean?" Ashley asked nervously.

Hex giggled.

"Wand!" barked Princess Poison.

EVA handed her the wand. Princess Poison muttered a spell:

**"Make this a dragon, fierce and cruel,
So Ashley hates her boarding school!"**

Green light shot out of Princess Poison's wand and hit the bronze statue, turning it green.

ROAR!

The statue suddenly sprang to life, becoming a huge dragon with shiny red scales, wings and a long tail. The dragon roared again and breathed out flames. Pawing the pedestal with its clawed feet, it looked ready to pounce.

"Oh dear," said Princess Poison. "The school mascot doesn't look very welcoming, does he?"

Because of Princess Poison's magic, no one else noticed what she had done, but Ashley was rooted to the spot in terror.

"Ashley!" urged Rory. "It's your turn. You need to walk through the gates."

"Can you make the dragon go away?" Ashley whispered to Mia and Charlotte.

"I'm sorry, we can't," Charlotte replied. "We've used up all our magic."

"I can't do it," said Ashley. "The dragon will get me."

"No, it won't," said Mia.

"How do you know?" asked Ashley, her voice quavering.

"Because we've met dragons before," said Mia. "At a place called Wishing Star Palace."

"They look scary, but dragons are actually friendly," said Charlotte.

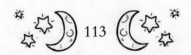

The dragon spread its wings and let out another fiery roar.

"You've got to trust us," said Mia. "You can't let Princess Poison spoil this moment for you."

"It won't hurt you," said Charlotte. "I promise."

Taking a deep breath, Ashley walked through the gates towards the dragon.

"She's being really brave," Mia said as they watched Ashley reach the end of the path.

The dragon stared at Ashley with glittering green eyes, flicking its tail.

"Go on," prompted one of the students. "Pat the dragon!"

Squeezing her eyes shut, Ashley reached
out a trembling hand and patted the
dragon's head.

"Yay!" cheered the students. Someone
handed Ashley a glowing lantern and said,
"Welcome to Dearborn Academy."

Ashley opened her eyes, and her face was
flooded with relief.

Zoe gave her a hug. "Way to go, roomie!"

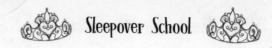
Mia and Charlotte went over to the dragon. Mia stroked its scales.

"I know you're really very gentle," said Charlotte. "But would you mind doing us a favour?" She leaned in and whispered something in the dragon's ear.

Giving a mighty roar, the dragon leaped

off its pedestal and ran out of the gates – right at Princess Poison, Hex and EVA!

"Aaaggghhh! Run!" shrieked Princess Poison, sprinting away as fast as her high heels could carry her.

Hex charged after her, his short legs struggling to keep up.

"COMMAND NOT RECOGNISED!" said EVA, wheeling around in circles.

"Are you feeling happier now?" Mia asked Ashley when the ceremony was over.

Ashley nodded, beaming. "I really like it here," she said. "Everyone is so friendly. I feel like I fit in already."

Suddenly, all of the lanterns magically changed colour. They glowed pink, violet, blue, orange and green, lighting up the night with every colour of the rainbow.

The dragon flew back to the pedestal, folded
its wings and became a statue once more,
but now it had ruby-red scales and emeralds
for eyes.

"That's so beautiful!" said Ashley,
astonished.

"It's because we granted your wish,"
explained Charlotte.

As Ashley ran off to join Zoe, Charlotte
felt a tap on her shoulder. Turning around,
she saw Princess Ella.

"Congratulations, girls," said Ella. "I guess
the Lucky Owl did bring you good luck. I
was so proud of you for remembering that
dragons are gentle." She touched her wand
to each of their necklaces and a second

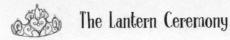

moonstone appeared in their pendants.

"Now we're halfway to earning our moonstone bracelets," said Mia.

"And halfway to getting Luna's magic back," said Charlotte, fighting back a yawn.

"You two must be exhausted," said Ella. "It's time for you to go home."

"Can we just say goodbye to Ashley first?" said Mia.

They found Ashley chatting with her new friends.

"We've got to go now," Charlotte told Ashley. "But good luck at school."

"Thanks so much for everything," said Ashley. "It's been an amazing adventure – just like in *The Magic Boarding School*."

"Hopefully real boarding school will be even more fun than it is in books," said Mia.

"I know it will be," Ashley replied, smiling.

After they had said goodbye, the girls

returned to Princess Ella.

"See you soon, Mia," said Charlotte, hugging her best friend.

"To grant another tiara star wish!" said Mia, her blue eyes sparking.

Ella waved her

wand and the magic whisked them away. A moment later, Charlotte was back in her bedroom wearing her own pyjamas. As she climbed into bed, there was a soft knock on her bedroom door.

Her mum came in, wearing a smart suit and holding her briefcase. "Did you have a good day, sweetie?" she said, perching on the edge of Charlotte's bed.

"It was better than good," said Charlotte, as her mum tucked her in, "it was magical!"

The End

Join Charlotte and Mia in their next Secret Princesses adventure

Read on for a sneak peek!

Pet Rescue

I can't wait to eat these!" said Mia Thompson, measuring out a spoonful of baking powder and adding it to a mixing bowl. She and her little sister, Elsie, were trying out a new chocolate brownie recipe that Mia had found online.

"What can I do?" Elsie asked.

"You can add the chocolate," said Mia.

Elsie poured a cup of chocolate chips into the bowl and Mia stirred them into the dark brown mixture.

"They're ready to bake now," said Mia, carefully spooning it into a baking tin.

The girls' mum opened the oven door and slid the baking tray inside. "How long do they need to cook for?" she asked.

Mia went over to the laptop computer on the kitchen table. She checked the recipe that was on the screen. "Thirty minutes," she told her mum.

PING! As she clicked the recipe tab shut, Mia heard the sound of a new email arriving. It was from her best friend, Charlotte!

Clicking the email open, Mia read the message:

Hey Mia,

I thought you might like this super cute kitten video. Hope to see you soon. ;-)

Lots of love,

Charlotte

xxx

"Mum!" called Mia. "Charlotte sent me a video. Can I watch it?"

Read Pet Rescue to find out what happens next!

Midnight Feast Menu

At your next sleepover party, you can have a midnight feast just like Ashley and her boarding school friends. Serve your feast with hot chocolate or bubbly ginger beer!

Mini Pizzas (serves 4)

First, something savoury to start off your feast.

Make sure to ask a grown-up for help when using the oven.

Ingredients:
4 white muffins
a jar of tomato pasta sauce
225g grated mozzarella cheese
16 slices of pepperoni

Instructions:
1. Preheat the oven to 190°C
2. Split the muffins in half and arrange them cut side up on a baking tray
3. Spoon tomato sauce over each muffin half
4. Top with cheese and pepperoni slices
5. Bake for ten minutes, or until the cheese is melted and lightly browned

Fab Fridge Cake

Don't forget dessert! It will help you have sweet dreams!

Ingredients:
- 100g butter
- 25g soft brown sugar
- 3 tbsp cocoa
- 4 tbsp golden syrup
- 225g digestive biscuits, crushed
- 150g raisins or mini marshmallows
- 225g milk chocolate

Top tip:
Remember to brush your teeth after your midnight feast!

Instructions:
1. Add the butter, sugar, cocoa and golden syrup to a bowl. Microwave for a couple of minutes until melted

2. Add the crushed biscuits, raisins or marshmallows and mix well

3. Press the mixture into a 20cm square greased tin

4. Melt 225g milk chocolate. Pour it on top and smooth it over the mixture

5. Mark into squares and chill in the fridge for at least an hour before cutting. Enjoy!

Secret PRINCESSES

What would you wish for?

Are you a Secret Princess?

Join the Secret Princesses Club at:

secretprincessesbooks.co.uk

Explore the magic of the
Secret Princesses and discover:

♥ Special competitions! ♥
♥ Exclusive content! ♥
♥ All the latest princess news! ♥

Secret
PRINCESSES

Special thanks to Anne Marie Ryan
For Cathie Bitter, Shannon Canavin,
Dawn Peters and Deanne Cicerchia, my
amazing high school friends

ORCHARD BOOKS

First published in Great Britain in 2018 by The Watts Publishing Group

1 3 5 7 9 10 8 6 4 2

Text copyright © Hothouse Fiction, 2018
Illustrations copyright © Orchard Books, 2018

A CIP catalogue record for this book
is available from the British Library.

ISBN 978 1 40835 099 7

Printed and bound in Great Britain by Clays Ltd, St Ives plc

The paper and board used in this book are made from wood from responsible sources.

Orchard Books
An imprint of
Hachette Children's Group
Part of The Watts Publishing Group Limited
Carmelite House
50 Victoria Embankment
London EC4Y 0DZ

An Hachette UK Company
www.hachette.co.uk
www.hachettechildrens.co.uk

Series created by Hothouse Fiction
www.hothousefiction.com